THE PRINCESS AND THE FROG

Tiana's Cookbook

Recipes for Kids

DISNEY PRESS

New York

Dear Reader,

From the time I was little, I loved cooking. I remember my daddy stirring up a big pot of gumbo with whatever he had in the cupboard. I swear just about every neighbor we had would come visit as soon as they caught a whiff. His food always brought people together and made them happy.

One day, my daddy told me his secret ingredient, the one that he sprinkled in everything: love. Now, I'm a practical girl, and I know the regular ingredients are really important. But even though it may sound corny, it's true: if you don't put your heart into a dish, it won't come out the way you want.

This book of recipes includes all my favorites—from real New Orleans jambalaya to mud pie I named in honor of my friend Ray. I rated the recipes on a five-frog scale: 🐸🐸🐸🐸. That way, you'll know whether you're about to cook something easy (🐸) or complicated (🐸🐸🐸🐸).

Here are a few things to remember:

- 🐾 Before you start, be sure to wash your hands, put on an apron, and pull your hair back.

- 🐾 Always ask a grown-up for help when using mixers, blenders, stoves, ovens, and knives.

- 🐾 Never touch a hot stove!

- 🐾 Cooking meat can be tricky—you have to make sure it's cooked through or you could get sick. Always ask an adult to help you check when it's done.

- 🐾 Remember to clean up.

- 🐾 Don't forget to add the secret ingredient!

I hope you have as much fun making these dishes as I do.

—Princess Tiana

Table of Contents

Big Easy Breakfasts

Tiana's Famous Beignets

Makes 14 to 16

You know you're in New Orleans if the doughnuts are square and don't have holes. These pillow-shaped French pastries are called *beignets*.

INGREDIENTS:

3 cups flour
$1/3$ cup sugar
2 teaspoons baking powder
$1/2$ teaspoon baking soda

$1/2$ teaspoon salt
$1/2$ teaspoon nutmeg
1 cup buttermilk
$1/3$ cup water

1 egg, beaten
$1/2$ teaspoon vanilla extract
Vegetable oil, for frying
Confectioners' sugar, for dusting

DIRECTIONS:

1. In a medium bowl, combine $2\frac{3}{4}$ cups of the flour with the sugar, baking powder, baking soda, salt, and nutmeg. Whisk everything together.

2. In a large bowl, whisk together the buttermilk, water, egg, and vanilla extract. Stir in the flour mixture from Step 1.

3. Use some of the remaining flour to dust your work surface. Place the dough on it and pat it into a large $1/2$-inch-thick square. Dust the top with more flour if it gets sticky. Next, slice the dough into $2\frac{1}{2}$-inch squares.

4. Now it's time to fry the beignets—be sure to ask an adult to help you! Heat 2 inches of vegetable oil in a heavy saucepan on the stovetop until the temperature reaches 325° on a deep-fat thermometer. Check the temperature every so often while cooking. If it gets too hot, temporarily turn the heat down, or off.

5. Carefully drop 3 dough squares at a time into the hot oil. Fry them for 3 minutes, turn them over, and continue frying for 3 more minutes. Use a slotted spoon to transfer the beignets to a wire rack set atop paper towels to drain. Dust the beignets with confectioners' sugar, and enjoy!

 **TIP** Use a sifter or a small sieve to put the sugar on the top of the beignets.

Egg in a Nest 🐸🐸🐸
Serves 1

Here's a fun-to-cook breakfast that's as sunny as the South—an egg fried right inside a slice of toast.

INGREDIENTS:

1 egg
1 slice bread
1 tablespoon butter

DIRECTIONS:

1. Crack the egg by striking it against the rim of a bowl. Hold the shell above the bowl and carefully pull it apart. Pick out any shell fragments that may have fallen into the bowl along with the egg.

2. Use a 3-inch cookie cutter to cut a shape out of the center of the bread slice.

3. Melt the butter in a frying pan over medium heat. Place the bread in the pan and fry it lightly on one side for 1 to 2 minutes. You can also fry the cutout shape. Use a spatula to flip the bread over. Reduce the heat to low.

4. Carefully pour the egg into the cutout hole. Cover the pan and cook until the egg has set in the bread "nest," about 3 minutes. For an over-easy egg, flip the bread and egg, and cook it for another minute or so. Transfer it to a plate with the spatula.

 **TIP** For a fun "nest," use a cookie cutter shaped like a heart, a star, or a flower instead of a round one.

Charlotte's Coffee Cake 🍁🍁🍁🍁

Serves 10 to 12

Charlotte loves surprises and when she first bit into this she got a good one. There's cinnamon streusel swirled through the middle.

INGREDIENTS:

Butter for greasing the baking pan

Cinnamon Filling:
$1/3$ cup brown sugar
4 tablespoons softened butter
2 tablespoons flour
1 tablespoon cinnamon

Coffee Cake:
3 cups flour
2 teaspoons baking powder
$1/2$ teaspoon baking soda
$1/2$ teaspoon salt
$1 1/2$ cups sugar

$1/2$ cup butter, softened
3 eggs
2 teaspoons vanilla extract
16-ounce container sour cream
Confectioners' sugar, for dusting

DIRECTIONS:

1. Heat the oven to 350°. Grease a 12-cup Bundt pan, making sure you get into all the grooves.

2. Combine the ingredients for the cinnamon filling in a bowl and blend them with your fingertips until the mixture resembles coarse crumbs. In another bowl, combine the flour, baking powder, baking soda, and salt. Set both mixtures aside.

3. In a large bowl, use a wooden spoon to mix the sugar into the butter until soft and smooth. Beat in the eggs one at a time. Then beat in the vanilla extract and sour cream. Add the flour mixture a little at a time, beating well after each addition.

4. Spoon half of the coffee-cake batter into the Bundt pan and sprinkle the cinnamon filling on top. Pour in the remaining batter. Drag a butter knife back and forth through the batter to swirl in the cinnamon.

5. Bake the coffee cake for 50 to 60 minutes until a toothpick inserted in the center of the cake comes out clean. Let the cake cool in the pan for 10 minutes. Then ask an adult to help you invert it onto a wire rack to cool completely. Dust the top with confectioners' sugar.

Banana French Toast ♦♦♦

Serves 6

This French toast has a treat in the middle—sliced bananas.

INGREDIENTS:

1-pound loaf French or Italian
    bread, cut into thick slices
1 to 2 bananas, sliced
3 eggs

½ cup milk
1 to 2 tablespoons butter
1 to 2 tablespoons vegetable oil

DIRECTIONS:

1. First, cut a wide, deep slit down through the top crust of each bread slice. Stuff each pocket with 3 to 4 banana slices.

2. In a shallow dish or pie plate, whisk together the eggs and milk.

3. Heat the butter and oil in a large skillet over medium-high heat. Dip each bread slice in the egg mixture, turning it to coat both sides, and place it in the skillet.

4. Cook the French toast for 2 to 3 minutes on the first side until golden brown. Then use a spatula to flip the slices, and cook them for another 2 to 3 minutes. Serve with butter and maple syrup.

Yummy Lunches

Mama Odie's Muffuletta Sandwich ❧❧

Serves 4

Spread with garlicky chopped olives, this salami sandwich is popular in New Orleans, especially during Mardi Gras.

INGREDIENTS:

Muffuletta Spread:
5-ounce jar pimiento-stuffed green olives, drained and sliced
1 tomato, seeded and chopped
1 clove garlic, minced
1 teaspoon dried oregano
3 tablespoons olive oil
2 tablespoons balsamic vinegar
$\frac{1}{2}$ teaspoon ground black pepper

Sandwich:
9-inch round loaf of Italian bread
Olive oil
$\frac{1}{4}$ pound each of sliced baked ham, salami, Provolone cheese, and Monterey Jack or Swiss cheese

DIRECTIONS:

1. Combine all of the muffuletta spread ingredients in a bowl and stir until well mixed.

2. Slice the bread loaf in half lengthwise. Brush or drizzle the bottom piece with olive oil.

3. Layer on the meats, the cheeses, and the muffuletta spread, and then cover everything with the top half of the bread loaf.

4. Slice the sandwich into thick wedges.

Po' Boy Sandwich

Serves 1

This sandwich is traditionally made with roast beef and gravy, but you can substitute just about any lunch meat you like. If you want yours with lettuce, tomato, and mayonnaise, be sure to order it "dressed," as we say in New Orleans.

INGREDIENTS:

French roll or large hunk of French bread
Mayonnaise
Shredded lettuce

Tomato slices
Sliced roast beef
$\frac{1}{4}$ to $\frac{1}{2}$ cup warm beef gravy

DIRECTIONS:

1. Slice the roll or bread in half lengthwise and lightly toast both halves.

2. Spread mayonnaise on the bottom half of the roll. Layer on shredded lettuce, sliced tomatoes, and plenty of roast beef. Then spoon gravy on top of the roast beef.

3. Cover the sandwich with the top half of the roll and serve immediately.

PB & J Blossom Sandwiches

Serves 1

Shaped like flowers and filled with fruit jelly, these pretty little sandwiches are perfect for a picnic.

INGREDIENTS:

2 slices of bread
Peanut butter
Jelly

DIRECTIONS:

1. Using a flower-shaped cookie cutter, cut a flower shape from each slice of bread.

2. Use a water-bottle cap to cut a hole in the center of one of the flower shapes.

3. Spread the peanut butter and jelly on the whole flower shape. Then place the slice with the center hole on top.

Facilier's Fruit Salad

Serves 6

Dr. Facilier uses magic to stir up trouble, such as changing humans into frogs. But not all transformations require magic. With this recipe, for instance, all you need is fresh mint to turn a bowl of fruit into a fantastic salad.

INGREDIENTS:

4 cups cantaloupe or other melon balls
1 apple, cored and thinly sliced
$\frac{1}{2}$ pound grapes, halved

2 kiwis, peeled, quartered, and sliced
$\frac{1}{3}$ cup fresh mint sprigs

DIRECTIONS:

1. Combine the melon, apple, grapes, and kiwis in a large mixing bowl. Toss the fruit with a wooden spoon to evenly distribute the pieces.

2. Chop all but 2 or 3 of the mint sprigs. Toss the chopped mint into the salad and use the remaining sprigs for garnish.

 Before chopping mint or other fresh herbs, rinse them well and pat them dry.

Delicious Dinners

Jammin' Jambalaya ♣♣♣

Serves 6 to 8

Like many Cajun and Creole recipes, jambalaya is a delicious mix of seasoned meats and vegetables. One of the things that makes jambalaya different is that you stir raw rice right into the pot to simmer in the flavorful liquid.

INGREDIENTS:

2 tablespoons olive oil
2 boneless, skinless chicken breasts, cut into
   1-inch chunks
1/2 pound Andouille sausage, cooked and
   thinly sliced
1 medium onion, chopped
2 large celery stalks, chopped
1 small bell pepper, seeded and chopped
2 cloves garlic, peeled and chopped

1/4 teaspoon salt
1/8 teaspoon ground black pepper
1 cup canned chopped tomatoes,
   undrained
2 cups uncooked white rice
4 cups chicken broth
2 teaspoons Worcestershire sauce
1 teaspoon hot pepper sauce

DIRECTIONS:

1. Heat the oil in a large frying pan or pot over medium-high heat. Sauté the chicken until cooked through, about 5 minutes. Reduce the heat to medium.

2. Stir in the sausage, onion, celery, bell pepper, and garlic. Sprinkle on the salt and ground black pepper, and stir again. Cook the mixture for 5 minutes, stirring occasionally.

3. Stir in the chopped tomatoes and the uncooked rice. Then stir in the chicken broth. Bring the mixture to a boil.

4. Reduce the heat to low and cover the pan. Simmer the jambalaya until the rice is tender, about 20 minutes. Stir in the Worcestershire and hot pepper sauces.

 **TIP** If you like your food on the mild side, add less Worcestershire sauce and hot pepper sauce than the recipe calls for.

Yumbo Gumbo

Serves 4

It seems like everyone in New Orleans has their own gumbo recipe. This is my daddy's recipe—and my favorite.

INGREDIENTS:

1 cup all-purpose flour
1 teaspoon paprika
1 teaspoon ground thyme
1 teaspoon Old Bay seasoning
1 teaspoon salt
$\frac{1}{2}$ teaspoon cayenne pepper
2 quarts chicken stock

$\frac{1}{2}$ pound smoked sausage, sliced
1 cup onions, chopped
$\frac{1}{2}$ cup green bell peppers, chopped
$\frac{1}{2}$ cup celery, chopped
1 pound boneless, skinless chicken breasts, cut into cubes
1 pound shrimp, peeled and deveined
4 all-beef wieners, cut in $\frac{1}{2}$-inch pieces

DIRECTIONS:

1. Mix flour, paprika, thyme, Old Bay seasoning, salt, and pepper. Place mixture in a small pan. Bake in 350° oven until brown, stirring often. Set aside.

2. Place chicken stock in a 5 to 6 quart pot. Add smoked sausage, onions, bell peppers, and celery. Bring to a boil. Lower heat and simmer for 15 minutes.

3. Place spice mixture in a bowl. Stir in 1 cup water and mix until you have a smooth paste.

4. Slowly add paste to chicken stock, stirring constantly. Add chicken, shrimp, and wieners. Cook until chicken and shrimp are done, about 15 minutes. Serve over rice.

Red Beans and Rice 🍁🍁🍁

Serves 6 to 8

Flavored with crumbled bacon and sausage left over from Sunday dinner, this traditional Louisiana dish has long been a popular Monday special at New Orleans restaurants, including mine.

INGREDIENTS:

2 tablespoons olive oil
1 medium onion, chopped
1 large celery stalk, chopped
1 small bell pepper, seeded and chopped
3 scallions, chopped
2 tablespoons chopped parsley
2 cans (15 ounces each) kidney beans with the juice

1 can (14.5 ounces) chopped tomatoes
½ pound Andouille sausage, cooked and thinly sliced
4 slices bacon, cooked and crumbled
1½ teaspoons Worcestershire sauce
¼ teaspoon cayenne pepper
3 cups cooked white rice

DIRECTIONS:

1. Heat the oil in a large frying pan over medium heat. Add the onion, celery, bell pepper, scallions, and parsley to the pan and sauté them for 4 to 5 minutes, stirring occasionally.

2. Add the beans, tomatoes, sausage, bacon, Worcestershire sauce, and cayenne pepper to the vegetables, and stir until the ingredients are evenly mixed. Cover the pan and simmer the mixture for 30 minutes, stirring occasionally.

3. Serve the beans over white rice.

Cal's Chicken and Biscuits 🐦🐦🐦🐦

Serves 6 to 8

Comfort food was always on the menu at Cal's diner. This was one of his most popular dishes.

INGREDIENTS:

Filling:
4 tablespoons butter
1 cup finely chopped onion
1 stalk celery, chopped
$\frac{1}{3}$ cup flour
$1\frac{1}{2}$ cups chicken broth
$1\frac{1}{2}$ cups milk
$\frac{1}{2}$ teaspoon each of dried sage and dried thyme
$2\frac{1}{2}$ cups diced cooked chicken

2 cups cooked peas, carrots, or corn (or a mix of these)
Salt and pepper to taste
Biscuit Topping:
2 cups flour
1 tablespoon baking powder
$\frac{1}{2}$ teaspoon salt
$\frac{1}{4}$ cup cold butter, cut into $\frac{1}{4}$-inch pieces
$\frac{3}{4}$ cup milk

DIRECTIONS:

1. Melt the butter for the filling over medium heat in a large ovenproof pot. Stir in the onion and celery. Put a lid on the pan and cook for 7 to 8 minutes, stirring occasionally. Then stir in the flour.

2. Whisk the broth into the pan. When it starts to thicken, whisk in the milk. Add the sage, thyme, chicken, and peas or carrots or corn. Continue cooking and stirring for 5 to 7 minutes. Add salt and pepper to taste.

3. Remove the pan from the stove top and heat the oven to 375°. Meanwhile, make the biscuit topping by combining the flour, baking powder, and salt in a bowl. Use your fingertips to rub in the butter. Pour in the milk and stir just until the dough pulls together.

4. Turn the dough onto a floured surface and knead it 2 or 3 times with floured hands. Pat the dough into a $\frac{1}{2}$-inch-thick disk. Using a small cookie cutter, cut out dough circles and place as many as will fit, barely touching, on the filling.

5. Bake until the biscuits brown and the filling bubbles, about 20 to 30 minutes. Let it cool for 10 minutes before serving.

Buford's Fish Fillets 🍁🍁🍁

Serves 4

As the short-order cook at Duke's, Buford made this popular breaded-fish dish a lot. It tastes great dipped in ketchup or tartar sauce.

INGREDIENTS:

Vegetable oil for the baking pan
4 tablespoons butter
$\frac{2}{3}$ cup crushed buttery crackers (such as Ritz)
$\frac{1}{4}$ cup grated Parmesan cheese

$\frac{1}{2}$ teaspoon dried basil
$\frac{1}{2}$ teaspoon dried oregano
$\frac{1}{4}$ teaspoon garlic powder
1 pound sole, scrod, perch, or other mild fish fillets

DIRECTIONS:

1. Heat the oven to 350°. Grease a 9 x 13-inch baking pan and set it aside.

2. Melt the butter in a saucepan over low heat. Then pour it into a mixing bowl. In a pie pan, stir together the crushed crackers, grated cheese, basil, oregano, and garlic powder.

3. Place the fish fillets in the melted butter. Turn the fillets over so that both sides are coated. One at a time, dip the fish fillets in the crumb mixture, again coating both sides, and place them in the baking pan.

4. Bake the fish until it flakes apart when you insert a fork, about 20 to 25 minutes.

Duke's Macaroni and Cheese ❦❦❦

Serves 6 to 8

Layered with American and cheddar cheese and sprinkled with buttery cracker crumbs, this is a favorite at Duke's.

INGREDIENTS:

1 pound elbow macaroni, cooked according
    to the package directions
Butter for greasing the baking pan
3 cups half-and-half or whole milk
12 to 18 slices total, American or cheddar cheese
12 buttery crackers (such as Ritz)
Salt, pepper, and paprika to taste

DIRECTIONS:

1. Heat the oven to 350°. Grease a 13 x 9–inch baking pan or large casserole dish.

2. Spoon a third of the cooked macaroni into the pan. Pour in 1 cup of the half-and-half or milk. Then cover everything with 4 to 6 slices of the cheese. Add two more layers of pasta, half-and-half or milk, and cheese.

3. Place the crackers in a sealable plastic bag and crush them with your fingers or a rolling pin. Add the salt, pepper, and paprika to the cracker crumbs. Sprinkle the crumbs on top of the pasta and cheese. Bake until bubbly, about 35 to 45 minutes.

Down-Home Breads, Sides & Drinks

Skillet Cornbread ❦❦❦

Serves 8 to 10

This slightly sweetened quick bread is a cinch to whip up, and there's hardly a southern supper it doesn't go well with. It makes a tasty breakfast, too, served warm with butter and honey.

INGREDIENTS:

3 tablespoons butter
1 cup flour
1 cup fine yellow cornmeal

2 tablespoons sugar
1 teaspoon baking soda
1 teaspoon baking powder

$\frac{1}{2}$ teaspoon salt
2 large eggs, lightly beaten
2 cups buttermilk

DIRECTIONS:

1. Heat the oven to 400°. Use a pat of the butter to grease a 10-inch cast-iron skillet (or a 10-inch deep-dish pie pan). Melt the remaining butter in a small saucepan over low heat. Remove the pan from the stove and set it aside.

2. Sift the flour, cornmeal, sugar, baking soda, baking powder, and salt into a large bowl. In a separate bowl, whisk together the eggs and buttermilk. Pour the melted butter into the buttermilk mixture.

3. Make a well in the dry ingredients and pour in the buttermilk mixture. Stir the batter just until evenly blended. Then pour it into the buttered skillet.

4. Bake the cornbread until a toothpick inserted into the center comes out clean, about 25 to 30 minutes. Cool the bread in the pan on a wire rack for 10 minutes before slicing it.

Naveen's Green Beans ✦✦✦

Serves 8

For Prince Naveen, a good veggie recipe has a lot in common with his favorite kind of music—it's all jazzed up.

INGREDIENTS:

2 pounds fresh green beans
1 cup sliced fresh
    mushrooms
½ cup diced onions

3 cloves garlic, minced
⅓ cup olive oil
1 can (8 ounces) water
    chestnuts, drained

½ teaspoon dried basil
½ teaspoon Italian seasoning
Salt and pepper to taste

DIRECTIONS:

1. Wash and trim the beans, then snap them in half. Place the beans in a saucepan with enough water to cover them. Bring the water to a boil, then reduce the heat and simmer the beans until just barely tender, about 8 minutes.

2. Drain the beans and immediately rinse them in cold water to stop the cooking process. Set them aside.

3. Sauté the mushrooms, onions, and garlic in the olive oil until tender, about 5 minutes. Add the water chestnuts, basil, Italian seasoning, and salt and pepper. Stir in the green beans and cook the mixture for 3 to 4 minutes to heat it through.

 **TIP** Garlic cloves are easier to peel and chop if you crush them first with a rolling pin.

Oven-Baked Potato Wedges 🐸🐸

Serves 4

These chunky wedges are like french fries, but instead of being fried, they crisp up in the oven.

INGREDIENTS:

4 medium Idaho potatoes
$\frac{1}{4}$ cup olive oil
Salt to taste

DIRECTIONS:

1. Heat the oven to 425°. Peel the potatoes and slice them into about 10 wedges. Dry off any excess starch with paper towels.

2. In a baking dish, toss the potatoes with the oil to coat them. Bake the potatoes for 25 minutes, turning them at least once. Sprinkle on salt.

Swamp-Water Smoothie

Serves 1

Whether you're dodging Cajun frog-hunters in a Louisiana swamp or lying low on a steamy summer day, this frosty fruit drink will help you keep your cool!

INGREDIENTS:

$\frac{1}{2}$ cup fresh orange juice
$\frac{1}{2}$ cup nonfat yogurt
$\frac{1}{4}$ cup blueberries, washed
1 frozen banana

DIRECTIONS:

1. Measure all of the ingredients into a blender and put the top on.

2. Blend on the puree setting until smooth, about 30 seconds or so.

 **TIP** Chopping the banana into pieces before freezing it will make it easier to blend.

Minty Iced Tea 🍁🍁
Serves 4

A hint of maple syrup is the secret to this old-time thirst quencher.

INGREDIENTS:

3 bags peppermint tea
1 quart near-boiling water
2 bags green tea
Maple syrup to taste
Ice

DIRECTIONS:

1. Steep the bags of peppermint tea in the water for 2 minutes. Add the bags of green tea and steep for 4 more minutes.

2. Remove the teabags and let the tea cool.

3. Stir in maple syrup to taste. Pour the tea into tall glasses filled with plenty of ice.

Juju's Juleps

Serves 6 to 7

Even Mama Odie's seeing-eye snake, Juju, knows how nice a sweet drink is on a sultry day in the bayou. This one combines lemon juice with the spicy fizz of ginger ale.

INGREDIENTS:

2 cups cold water
2/3 cup fresh lemon juice (about 2 lemons)
1/3 cup sugar
4 mint sprigs
1 quart ginger ale

DIRECTIONS:

1. Combine the water, lemon juice, sugar, and mint sprigs in a medium-size glass bowl. Let the mixture set for 30 minutes.

2. Strain the liquid into a serving pitcher. Pour in the ginger ale.

3. Serve the juleps over ice in tall glasses.

Dazzling Desserts

Big Daddy's Sugar Cookies 🍁🍁🍁🍁

Makes up to 4 dozen (depending on cookie size)

Since "Big Daddy" La Bouff is in the sugar business, these cookies are his favorite.

INGREDIENTS:

3 ½ cups flour
½ teaspoon salt
1 cup butter, softened

⅔ cup sugar plus more for sprinkling
1 large egg
1 tablespoon light corn syrup

1 tablespoon vanilla extract
Frosting and minicandies
   (optional)

DIRECTIONS:

1. Whisk together the flour and salt in a small bowl. Set it aside.

2. In a large bowl, use a wooden spoon to press the butter into the sugar until the mixture is soft and smooth. Stir in the egg, corn syrup, and vanilla extract. Then stir in the flour mixture from Step 1, one third at a time.

3. Divide the dough into two portions. Pat each portion into a disk, wrap it in plastic, and chill until firm enough to roll (1 to 2 hours).

4. Heat the oven to 375°. Working with one disk at a time, place the chilled dough between 2 sheets of waxed paper and roll it to about ¼-inch thickness. Use cookie cutters to cut out shapes from the dough. Reroll the dough scraps and cut out more shapes.

5. Place the shapes on an ungreased baking sheet, leaving an inch between them. If you're not planning to frost the cookies, sprinkle the tops with sugar.

6. Bake the cookies until light brown around the edges, 8 to 10 minutes. Then leave them on the baking sheet for a few minutes before transferring them to a wire rack to cool. Decorate the cooled cookies with frosting and minicandies, if you like.

Froggy-in-the-Water Cupcakes 🐸🐸

Makes 2 dozen

The swamp may be a great place to hang out if you're a frog, but you have to be on the lookout for hungry gators, just like the peepers on these cupcakes.

INGREDIENTS:

Blue food coloring
1 cup buttercream frosting
1 dozen baked cupcakes

12 large green gumdrops
2 dozen white chocolate chips
Black decorators' icing

DIRECTIONS:

1. Stir drops of food coloring into the frosting until you have a shade of watery blue. Frost the cupcakes.

2. For each cupcake, create a pair of frog eyes by slicing a gumdrop in half. Press a white chocolate-chip tip down into the cut surface of each gumdrop half, centering it near the bottom edge. Squirt a dab of black decorators' icing onto each chip.

3. Set the frog eyes on the cupcakes, gently pressing them partway into the frosting to hold them in place.

Ray's Mud Pie 🍁🍁
Serves 8

Not only is this chocolate dessert deep and thick as mud, it's every bit as sweet and irresistible as Ray, the firefly for whom it's named.

INGREDIENTS:

20 whole chocolate graham crackers
6 tablespoons melted butter
1 quart chocolate ice cream
½ cup chocolate fudge topping

½ cup semisweet chocolate chips
1 cup heavy cream
¼ cup powdered hot cocoa mix

DIRECTIONS:

1. Seal the graham crackers in a large plastic bag and crush them with a rolling pin until they resemble dirt. Stir 1½ cups of the crumbs into the melted butter. Pour the mixture into a 9-inch pie pan.

2. When the crumbs have cooled, press them against the bottom and sides of the pan to form the piecrust. Freeze the crust for 20 minutes.

3. Scoop half the ice cream into a bowl and let it soften for about 10 minutes. Then spread it in the chilled crust. Dig 8 holes in the ice cream and fill each with a tablespoon of fudge-topping "mud." Freeze the crust for another 10 minutes.

4. Stir chocolate chip "rocks" into the remaining ice cream, and then spread it over the pie. Return the pie to the freezer.

5. Beat the heavy cream at high speed for 3 to 5 minutes to thicken it. Add the cocoa mix and beat for 2 more minutes or so until the cream stiffens. Spread the whipped cream evenly over the pie and sprinkle on the remaining cracker crumbs. Wrap the pie in plastic and freeze it for 3 to 4 hours before serving.

 If you want to soften ice cream in a jiffy, try microwaving it for just a few seconds.

Louis's Alligator Cake 🐸🐸🐸
Serves 10 to 12

Inspired by Louis, the trumpet-playing gator, this playful cake is fun to make.

INGREDIENTS:

10-inch baked Bundt cake
1 can (16 ounces) white frosting
Green food coloring

Large marshmallow
4 malted milk balls
Gummy spearmint leaves

Green M&M'S candies
White-yogurt–covered pretzels

DIRECTIONS:

1. Cut the cake into 3 equal pieces. Slice one of the pieces in half at a 45-degree angle. Arrange the cake pieces on a tray or platter to create a curvy alligator body. Use one of the angled halves, placed cut-side down, for the tail. Slice the other angled half into 4 equal–size pieces for feet.

2. Stir drops of food coloring into the frosting until you have a deep shade of green. Frost the entire cake.

3. Cut the marshmallow in half and place the halves on the cake for eyeballs. Press a malted milk ball up against each eyeball for a pupil, using a dab of frosting to stick it in place. Press 2 more malted milk balls onto the alligator's snout for nostrils. Press gummy spearmint leaves and green M&M'S into the frosting along the body for scales, and add spearmint-leaf toes to each foot.

4. Lastly, break the yogurt-covered pretzels into pieces and stick them into the frosting along the front of the cake to create alligator teeth.

Berry Peachy Cobbler ❧❧❧

Serves 6 to 8

This is a cobbler with a twist. Instead of putting the filling under the crust, you spoon it on top. Then, as the cobbler bakes, the biscuit topping puffs up and over the bubbling fruit.

INGREDIENTS:

½ cup butter
3 cups sliced peaches (about
    4 large peaches)
1 cup raspberries
1 cup sugar

1 cup flour
2 teaspoons baking powder
Pinch of salt
1 cup milk

1 teaspoon vanilla extract
Whipped cream or ice cream,
    for topping

DIRECTIONS:

1. Heat the oven to 350°. Use a pat of the butter to grease a cast-iron skillet (or a 2 ½-quart casserole dish). Set the skillet aside. Melt the remaining butter in a saucepan over low heat. Remove the pan from the stove and set it aside.

2. Combine the peaches and raspberries in a medium bowl and sprinkle 1 tablespoon of the sugar over them. Gently stir the fruit and then set it aside.

3. In a separate bowl, whisk together the flour, baking powder, and salt. Add the remaining sugar, the milk, and the vanilla extract. Stir until the mixture is evenly blended.

4. Pour the melted butter into the batter and stir quickly but gently to mix it in. Immediately pour the batter into the skillet. Add the fruit with its juices, spooning it evenly into the pan and lightly pressing it partway into the batter with a spatula.

5. Bake the cobbler until the top is golden brown, about 1 hour. Serve warm with ice cream or whipped cream.

Bayou Bread Pudding ♣♣♣

Serves 8 to 10

Like most bread puddings, this one is flavored with cinnamon and nutmeg. But in New Orleans, bread pudding has a special ingredient: bits of juicy pineapple.

INGREDIENTS:

Butter for greasing the pan
9 cups dry French bread,
   in 1-inch cubes
1 cup pineapple cubes
$\frac{1}{2}$ cup raisins

1 teaspoon cinnamon
$\frac{1}{2}$ teaspoon nutmeg
Pinch of salt
3 cups milk
5 tablespoons butter

$\frac{1}{2}$ cup packed light brown sugar
3 large eggs
$\frac{1}{2}$ teaspoon vanilla extract
Caramel sauce or whipped cream

DIRECTIONS:

1. Heat the oven to 350°. Grease an 8-inch-square baking pan.

2. Combine the bread cubes, pineapple cubes, and raisins in a large mixing bowl. Sprinkle the cinnamon, nutmeg, and salt over the bread and fruit. Toss all the ingredients with a wooden spoon to mix them.

3. Combine the milk and butter in a medium saucepan and warm them over medium-low heat until the butter melts. Remove the pan from the heat and stir in the light brown sugar.

4. Pour the milk mixture over the bread and stir until all the cubes are moistened. Let the bread stand for 5 minutes to absorb the liquid.

5. In a small bowl, whisk together the eggs and the vanilla extract. Gently stir the eggs into the bread mixture.

6. Pour the pudding into the greased pan and bake it for 45 to 50 minutes. Serve the pudding warm, cut into squares, and topped with caramel sauce or whipped cream.

 **TIP** If the bread you're using isn't dry, toast the cubes lightly on a baking sheet in the oven before mixing them with the other ingredients.

ACKNOWLEDGMENTS

Many thanks to Deanna F. Cook at *Disney FamilyFun* magazine for her help with this project. This book would not have been possible without the recipes created by the talented staff of *Disney FamilyFun*.

Recipes edited by Cindy Littlefield, who also created the recipes on pages 6-7, 26-27, 30-31, and 62-63.

Photography by Joanne Schmaltz
except as follows—Jacqueline Hopkins: 10; Sandy Rivlin: 35

Food styling by Edwina Stevenson

"Yumbo Gumbo" recipe Copyright © 2009 Leah Chase. Reprinted by permission.

The movie *The Princess and the Frog* Copyright © 2009 Disney, story inspired in part by the book *The Frog Princess* by E. D. Baker Copyright © 2002, published by Bloomsbury Publishing, Inc.

Disney FamilyFun is a division of Disney Publishing Worldwide. For more great ideas and to subscribe to *Disney FamilyFun* magazine, visit FamilyFun.com or call 1-800-289-4849.

Special thanks to Simon Pearce for use of pottery, glassware, and other accessories on pages 4–6, 13–16, 19, 22, 24–26, 28, 38, 45, 47, 56, and 62. For more information, visit www.simonpearce.com or call 1-800-774-5277

Printed in the United States of America

Library of Congress Cataloging-in-Publication data on file.

ISBN 978-1-4231-2540-2

Visit www.disneybooks.com

First Edition

10 9 8 7 6 5 4 3 2

ILS NO G942-9090-6
307 2009

SUSTAINABLE FORESTRY INITIATIVE
Certified Fiber Sourcing
www.sfiprogram.org

For Text Pages Only